PARK HERE

In loving memory of Eva Lakin
and her Nanamobile—PL

Thanks to Andy,
for all the support and cups of tea—DT

Library of Congress Cataloging-in-Publication data is on file with the publisher.

Text copyright © 2020 by Patricia Lakin
Illustrations copyright © 2020 by Albert Whitman & Company
Illustrations by Daniel Tarrant
First published in the United States of America in 2020 by Albert Whitman & Company
ISBN 978-0-8075-6366-3 (hardcover)
ISBN 978-0-8075-6368-7 (ebook)

Printed in China
10 9 8 7 6 5 4 3 2 1 T&N 24 23 22 21 20 19

Design by Aphelandra Messer

For more information about Albert Whitman & Company,
visit our website at www.albertwhitman.com.

PARK HERE

Patricia Lakin

illustrated by
Daniel Tarrant

Albert Whitman & Company
Chicago, Illinois

Yes! I like the park!

PARK HERE

It's where I play.

I can race with friends all day.

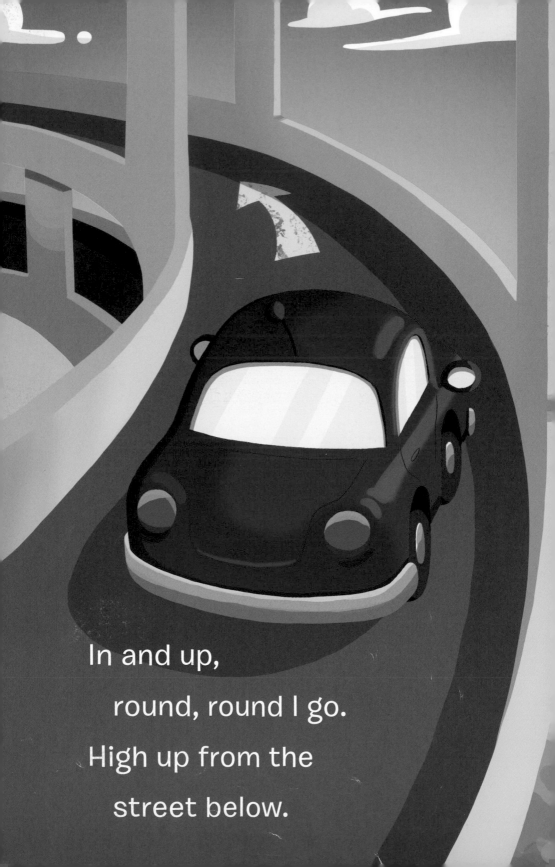

In and up,
round, round I go.
High up from the
street below.

I race out. What do I see?

No birds or grass
and not one tree.
Where are my friends,
the cars like me?

Oh good!
Big blocks!

One, two, I jump!

Oops! What's this?

I hit that bump!

Now here's a spot
where I can play.

But these fat posts

just block my way!

I cannot play here in the dark.

Where are my friends?
Where is the park?

Wait!

Do I hear a friendly shout?

Carl, can you please

help us out?

I zoom up. A happy sight!

Red cars, blue cars,
black and white!

We came in to race and play.
But we've been stuck here
this whole day!

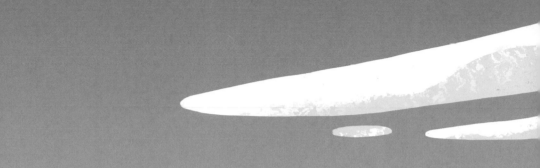

I look around. Now I know.

This is no park. We all must go!

Help us Carl.

We need some fun.

Turn your lights on,
one by one.

Zip! Zip! Zoom!
We race about.
With our lights,
we look for OUT.

I see the sign! O-U-T!

Come on friends.

Just follow me.

Down we go, two by two.

We are out.

We'll go with you.

The real park!
Hip, hip, hooray!